Text copyright © Eleanor Allen 1997
Illustrations copyright © Harvey Parker 1997

First published in Great Britain in 1997
by Macdonald Young Books

Reprinted in 2006 by Wayland,
an imprint of Hachette Children's Books

The right of Eleanor Allen to be identified as the
author and Harvey Parker the illustrator of this
Work has been asserted by them in accordance
with the Copyright, Designs and Patents Act 1988

Printed in China

British Library Cataloguing in Publication Data
available

ISBN-10: 0 7502 5032 1
ISBN-13: 978 0 7502 5032 0

Wayland
an imprint of Hachette Children's Books
338 Euston Road, London NW1 3BH

ELEANOR ALLEN

GHOST ON THE LANDING

Illustrated by Harvey Parker

WAYLAND

Chapter One

On the landing of the old house two children scuffled. The thick oak floorboards creaked and groaned beneath their feet, disturbing the dust of centuries.

The struggle was hard and mean, yet carried out in secretive silence. It was over quickly, for the pair were not evenly matched.

The girl, who was younger and lighter than the boy, was pushed against the banisters. Then she was forced to her knees, one arm twisted behind her back and the prize – a bag of sweets – was wrenched from her fingers.

The boy stuffed the sweets into his pocket and ran softly down the stairs without a backward glance.

Chapter Two

Louisa sat on the floor where Jack had pushed her. She felt full of fierce anger.

Jack was turning into a bully lately. Now he was breaking promises. Yesterday, in the car, he had promised their mother, "I'll be nice to Louisa while we're at Great-aunt Stella's".

Mum had gone away for three days, to visit Gran in hospital, believing him. Liar!

But Louisa couldn't complain about him, or make a fuss, and Jack knew it. For they were not really welcome in this tall old house. Uncle Richard was OK, but Aunt Stella did not like children. She had made that very plain. They must not be a nuisance to her. They must make themselves invisible, if possible.

Louisa clenched her fists. If Jack thought that meant he could bully her and get away with it, he had another think coming.

She would find some way to stop him.

"Revenge!" The word formed itself in Louisa's mind. She muttered it out loud.

"Revenge!" The word echoed round the landing space.
It breathed back to her from the walls.

She turned her head sharply. She thought she had sensed a movement.

A pale shaft of sunlight, heavy with swirling dust, was falling across the ancient floorboards. But beyond, the corners were full of gloom and shadows. Had one of those shadows moved?

Louisa felt her scalp prickling, like it does when you feel you are being watched.

She took hold of the banisters to pull herself up. In doing so, she noticed something strange.

At the very spot where
Jack had pushed her, the
banisters had been
repaired. There had
been a gap there once.

The gap was just the size to have been
made by something – or some*body* –
crashing through.

Louisa peered down through the
banisters into the dark stairwell. The old
staircase zigzagged round and round and
three floors below lay a patch of
flagstoned hall.

The drop was dizzyingly deep. Neck-breakingly deep!

With a frightened gasp, Louisa drew back. She scrambled to her feet and bolted down the stairs.

There was something spooky on that top landing, she told herself. Something more was moving up there than just the ancient dust.

Chapter Three

On the bottom flight of stairs, Louisa ran almost headlong into Aunt Stella's cleaning lady. She was on her hands and knees, rubbing at a mark on the stair carpet.

"Sorry," said Louisa, edging past.

From the hallway came a peculiar rasping sound.

She found Jack doubled over, choking.

He turned towards her, his face scarlet, his eyes watering and bulging. He waved his arms. Louisa stepped forward and thumped him on the back. He coughed and spluttered and something shot out of his mouth and landed on the rug.

It was one of the stolen sweets.

"Serves you right!" crowed Louisa. "That's my revenge, that is!"

Jack looked down at the bag of sweets, then threw it nastily against the wall. He pushed past her, knocking her deliberately against the hall table, and ran towards the kitchen.

Louisa picked up all the sweets. They had specks of dust and hairs from the rug sticking to them. They were only fit for the rubbish bin now.

At the bottom of the stairs she stopped
to stare in fascination at the grey, worn
flagstones and conjured up dreadful
pictures in her mind.

As her imagination dwelt on spooky
shadows and neck-breaking falls, an idea
began to weave itself inside her head.
An idea that formed itself into a plan –
a masterly plan to stop Jack bullying her.

Chapter Four

"Where's Jack?"

"In the garden," said Aunt Stella. "Go and join him, I'm cleaning the kitchen floor."

Louisa put on her anorak and found Jack in the garden, sulking.

The garden was long and narrow, like the house, with old, high, ivy-covered walls. The winter's morning was chilly and damp and the fruit trees and the bushes looked bare and miserable. The ground was muddy, with a covering of dank, rotting leaves.

"There's nothing to do out here," Jack grumbled.

He began to kick the leaves.

"You shouldn't do that," Louisa told him. "Insects live in leaves. You might crush something."

"You're *scared* of creepy-crawlies!" shouted Jack.

He kicked a pile of rotting leaves at Louisa. Then he began to scoop a pile up

in his hands.

"Don't you dare!" Louisa backed away. She imagined the slimy wetness of the leaves and things squirming and wriggling down her neck.

She turned and ran.

Clutching a handful of leaves, Jack chased after her.

Breathless, her heart thumping, Louisa turned on him.

"Stop it!" she shouted. "Stop bullying me, or I'll have my revenge on you – like I did with the sweets!"

"That wasn't revenge!" Jack shouted scornfully. "I just stuffed them into my mouth too fast. That's all!"

Louisa shook her head. She rolled her eyes and stared over Jack's shoulder towards the house. She pointed upwards, arm outstretched, towards the top storey. "It was the *curse of the top landing*," she said, in ghostly tones.

Jack laughed.

"There was a tragic accident up there, and the place is *haunted*!" said Louisa quickly. "That's why Aunt Stella didn't want us here. In case the presence of us children stirred up – some *other presence*!"

"Oo-oooh," scoffed Jack. "You've really got me scared!"

"Don't you want to know what happened? Don't you want to hear about the curse?" It was strange, but Louisa found she was starting to believe her own tale, even if Jack wasn't.

"No," said Jack, "I've got better things to do."

He dropped the leaves and wandered off, in search of better things. But the garden was boring and the weather bitterly cold. So when Louisa shouted that she was going back inside to carry out some ghostly investigations, Jack trailed after her.

Chapter Five

"This is the spot," whispered Louisa, pointing. "The very spot where the body fell. With a single, piercing scream, it plummeted three floors and landed THUMP! Come, stare up into the murky regions to where the tragic accident took place."

Silently, heads back, mouths open, they gazed up into the dark stairwell. Their imaginations ran wild.

A piercing scream rang out. It came from both of them. For out of the darkness two floors up a pale, white face was floating. A face that hovered over the banister rail and stared down at them, down, down, down. Louisa's heart seemed to have leaped right out. She thought of the body hurtling down, right on to the very spot where the two of them stood.

"Run, Jack!" she cried.

Jack sucked in breath. He grabbed her arm. "It's Mrs Whatshername!" he gasped. "It's only Mrs Whatshername ..."

Only the cleaning lady.

Sheepishly, they crept away.

Behind the kitchen door, Jack laughed and laughed. "I am the ghostly cleaning lady of the top landing." He raised his arms. "And if you don't get your filthy feet out of my hallway, I'll tip my dustpan over you!"

"You won't think it's so funny," muttered Louisa, "when the real ghost appears."

Chapter Six

"But there *is* a curse on the landing!" insisted Louisa when they went to bed that night. "Look at the banisters, if you don't believe me."

Jack examined them. "So they've been repaired," he said. "So what?"

"So I'll tell you how the tragedy happened," said Louisa. "Once upon a time, about a hundred years ago, there lived a girl and boy here, just like us.

Now that boy was always bullying the girl, just like you bully me. And one day, he ran at her to grab her sweets, but the girl ducked. The boy couldn't stop himself. He crashed into the banisters and fell straight through to meet his death in the hall below. And now there's a curse on the landing. And if any boy bullies a girl here, she can call for revenge, like I did this morning. And revenge will come."

"Oh yeah?" said Jack. He rushed off into Louisa's room and grabbed her old stuffed, saggy dog Barnaby.

"I'm taking Barnaby prisoner!" he cried.

"I can't sleep without Barnaby!"

"Then tell your ghostly friends to get him back!" he challenged. "Now let's see you get revenge!"

Chapter Seven

Louisa couldn't sleep without Barnaby. She tried and tried until even the terror of crossing the dark landing seemed worth the risk to rescue him.

The door to her uncle and aunt's room was ajar and their voices, especially Aunt Stella's, drifted out.

"It's not a suitable house for children. I shan't feel easy until they've gone," she was saying.

"But the tragedy happened long ago," said Uncle Richard.

"The house hasn't forgotten."

Louisa's eyes flew through the dimness to the banisters.

"The tragedy happened long ago!" So a tragedy really *had* happened.

Louisa's mouth turned so dry she could scarcely swallow.

"The house hasn't forgotten."

What if everything she thought she had imagined was true?

Even the revenge?

Louisa bolted for her bedroom, dived into bed and pulled the covers round her ears.

Barnaby remained a prisoner.

Chapter Eight

A voice cried out in the night. Jack was crying out in terror.

A door opened on the landing. A light clicked on and shone beneath Louisa's door. She heard Aunt Stella's voice, then Uncle Richard's. She leaped out of bed and scurried towards them.

Uncle Richard was struggling into his dressing-gown. Aunt Stella had hers on already. She shouldered open Jack's door and flicked on his light, as fast and fearless as the detectives on TV.

33

Jack was sitting up in bed, pale and shivering.

Aunt Stella heaved a sigh. Relief was peppered with annoyance. "What was all that racket for?"

Jack's eyes darted wildly round the room.

"I... I... I..." he stammered.

"Stop gibbering!" snapped Aunt Stella. "You've had a nightmare, lad, that's all."

"He looks very white," muttered Uncle Richard anxiously.

"He ate too much supper," said Aunt Stella. "Serves him right." She tugged Jack's duvet straight. "Now, perhaps we can all get back to bed."

Louisa saw panic in Jack's eyes at the thought of being alone. His panic spread to her. There was nothing out of the ordinary in the room now. But what if something *had* been there? What if something had moved around in the darkness, breathing revenge? Revenge for the capture of Barnaby?

The hairs on Louisa's arms stood on end and her knees began to tremble.

"Want Louisa to stay a minute…" mumbled Jack.

"Then don't hang about catching cold,
Louisa. And don't forget to put
the light out."

Jack flung Louisa the oddest look.
Accusing, scared, angry? All those things –
and more – in a single look.

"Was it just a nightmare, Jack?" asked
Louisa fearfully.

"I suppose you think it's your rotten
revenge," he hissed. "I suppose you think
your ghost friends haunted me?" Jack's
eyes looked dark and wild.

Louisa swallowed. She glanced nervously around. "D-did they, Jack?"

"Course not, stupid! Because they don't exist. I ate too much supper. I had a nightmare, like Aunt Stella said. Your stupid revenge is a load of rubbish!"

Louisa felt flooded with relief. But she didn't let him see.

Instead she said challengingly, "Sure about that?"

"Yeah."

"Night then." Louisa clicked off Jack's light.

"And you can take that stupid dog with you," he called, trying to sound off-hand.

Louisa took Barnaby and cuddled him close.

As she closed the door, Louisa heard, "I'm sorry," muttered reluctantly.

And then Jack gave a sigh. Just a little sigh. But it sounded like a sigh of relief that he had apologized and that Barnaby had gone.

And that the revenge had stopped?

Chapter Nine

Louisa never found out what really happened to Jack, the night he kidnapped Barnaby. But he seemed to have learned a lesson, for he didn't bully her again.

They both avoided the top landing, if they could. And they always ran quickly down the stairs and never hung about in the hall. They were polite, but very quiet, as though they were holding their breath, afraid of drawing attention to themselves. Afraid of more than Aunt Stella. Afraid that if they spoke too loudly, or argued or squabbled, something might hear and seek revenge.

Mum arrived at last to take them home and they were eager to be gone.

When Uncle Richard went upstairs to collect their stuff, Louisa went with him. She wanted to ask a question.

"Uncle Richard, you know those banisters?" she said. "How did they break?"

"They didn't," he said. "They got woodworm and turned so rotten they weren't safe. So I took them out and replaced them.

"*You* did?"

"Yes, why?"

"Nothing. I just wondered."

Louisa looked down into the stairwell with a puzzled frown.

No tragic fall. No neck-breaking crash on to the flagstones. No spooky shadows on the landing and no revenge.

Just my own imagination, she thought. And ideas she had put in Jack's. Yet it had seemed so real.

"Bye-bye!"

"Bye!"

"Thank you for having us! Oh – and please say goodbye to Mrs Whatshername – your cleaning lady – for us," shouted Louisa through the car window.

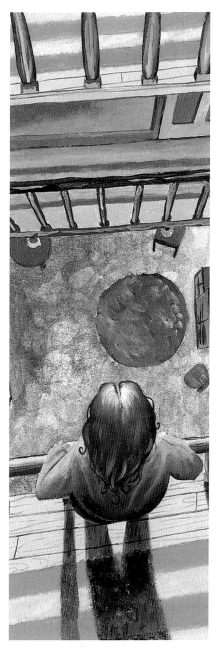

Aunt Stella's smile shrivelled into a lip-tremble of alarm. One hand flew to her chest.

"W–we..." she stammered. Then, strangely, she looked at Uncle Richard, as though asking for help.

Uncle Richard sadly, but firmly, shook his head.

"We have no cleaning lady, dear," he said.

Louisa pictured Mrs Whatshername, always on the stairs, always in the same place, cleaning the same dark stain on the carpet; but it was Aunt Stella who scrubbed the kitchen floor and cleaned the windows and vacuumed and dusted all the rooms. Mrs Whatshername, whose pale, pale face had appeared over the banisters of the stairwell in the gloom, scaring them half to death.

And a chill as icy cold as a breath from the North Pole went through her.

"You *have* got a cleaning lady!" cried Jack, quite fiercely. "She's always on your stairs!"

"Shh, Jack," she croaked. "I'll explain to you later."

"Explain what?" he demanded, as they drove away.

"About the *real* ghost on the landing," whispered Louisa.

If you have enjoyed this book, why not try these other creepy titles:

The Claygate Hound by Jan Dean
It's the school trip to Claygate, and Zeb and Ryan are ready to explore, until they hear stories about the ghost in the woods. It all sounds like a stupid story. But then the boys start to see shadows moving in the trees and eyes glistening in the darkness. Could the Claygate Hound really exist?

The Ghosts of Golfhawk School by Tessa Potter
Martin and Dan like to scare others with stories about the ghosts at Golfhawk School. But when Kirsty arrives and strange things start to happen it no longer seems a joke. Can she really see ghostly figures in the playground? And why have students and teachers started to get sick?

Beware the Wicked Web by Anthony Masters
Where had the enormous, dusty spider's web come from? The sticky, silky folds had filled the attic room, and were now clinging to Rob and Sam as they explored the room. In the centre of the web was a huge egg, which was just about to hatch…

Danny and the Sea of Darkness by David Clayton
When does a dream become reality? Danny wakes one night to find himself out at sea during a terrible storm. As he falls overboard into the icy water Danny wonders if he will ever return from the Sea of Darkness.

Time Flies by Mary Hooper
The large oak box looked like the perfect place to hide, but Lucy could never have imagined what powers lay inside. Lucy steps back in time to a strange and scary world. Can she find her way home again before it's too late?